Lizzie McGuire

My secret Journal

Based on the series created by Terri Minsky

New York

Text by Christien Haywood

Printed in Singapore

First Edition

1 3 5 7 9 10 8 6 4 2

Library of Congress Catalog Card Number: 2002093171

ISBN: 0-7868-3432-3

For more Disney Press fun, visit www.disneybooks.com

Visit DisneyChannel.com

Monday

Dear Journal,

First page . . . what to write? Hmmmm . . . Well, I'm sitting here on my bed, attempting to digest my mother's tuna noodle casserole and thinking about this past week. It was my first official week in junior high—and it was totally cool. Everything went totally well—

Um . . . okay . . . I can't do this. What I just wrote was totally bogus. I mean, this is my own private journal, right? So nobody else is going to read this. So there's totally no reason to be anything but honest. And honestly, this whole junior high thing is freaking me out.

I guess the problem is I'm worrying too much about not fitting in. What I _should_ be thinking about is all the awesome things ahead of me at Hillridge this year (cool clubs, dances, seriously cute boys). I _should_ be way psyched, not freaking over whether or not my hair has become a museum-worthy collection of split ends.

C'mon, what am I so worried about? Whatever happens this year, good or bad, I know exactly what's gonna get me through it—my very best friends in the whole entire world. . . .

My Very Best Friends in the Whole Entire World!

Miranda (Miranda isabelle Sanchez)

Bottom line: if your best friends are with you, it's a good hair day.

She's super loyal, super cool, super brave, and totally fun to be with. She's also super blunt, but in a "true friend" kinda way.

Like, not every friend would actually pull you aside and let you know you walked out of the girls' room with ten inches of toilet paper stuck to your platform shoe (which actually happened my first official day in junior high—real smooth, huh?).

Miranda's family is from Mexico—and I love eating dinner at her house (tamale heaven). As far as fashion, Miranda's got slammin' style. She especially loves wearing a "British invasion" Union Jack design and even worked it into one of her cool nail creations (manicurandas rock!).

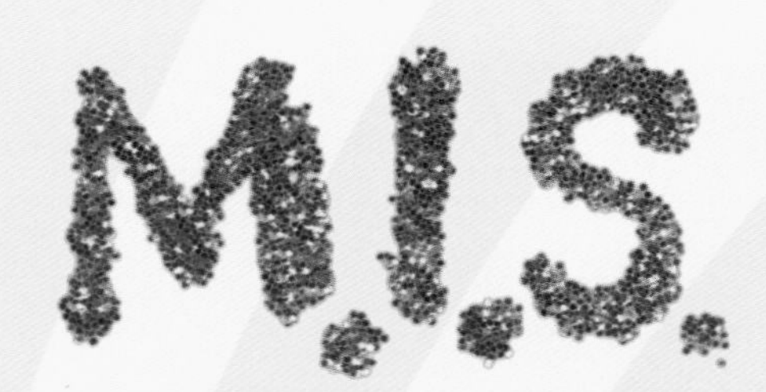

Gordo (David Zephyr Gordon)

He's really clever, really funny, really thoughtful, and really smart. If you want to know anything about movie trivia, weird hobbies, world cultures, or ancient music (like, from 1945), he's your go-to guy. That's _if_ you want to know about that stuff!

Gordo's family is Jewish, and last year at Hanukkah, he invited me and Miranda over to his house for dinner and we had some great food (Gordo says he totally OD's on the potato pancakes every year, and I can see why—they're dee-lish!).

At school, Gordo's got really strong opinions, and he doesn't care whether the other kids agree or not. He doesn't like being a part of what he calls "group think."

Like this past week, I saw a poster for cheerleading tryouts and mentioned I was thinking of signing up—but Gordo totally hates the idea. He said any group that forces you to be cheerful is, by nature, evil. Weird, right?

Sometimes I really don't get Gordo. And his fashion sense is . . . well, pretty much nonexistent. But, fashion flops aside, I have to say that _most_ of the time, I think Gordo is just about the best guy friend a girl could ever have.

Potato pancakes from last year's Hanukkah dinner at Gordo's house. Yum!

My Home Life

The 'Rents

Mom (Jo McGuire)

Put on this earth to make me die of embarrassment. Like the time she came into my room pretending to be looking for a hairbrush, then pulled out the mother-daughter handbook and turned to those chapters about "becoming a young woman."

Then there's dropping me off right in front of Ethan Craft while yelling things like, "Don't forget to bring home those dirty gym clothes again!" Sigh. She'd be unbearable if she wasn't such a great mom.

Dad (Sam McGuire)

My dad can be pretty embarrassing, too. For one thing, he freely admits he was a Mathlete and president of his Audio-Visual Club when he was in school—and he's got the geeky yearbook picture to prove it. And then there's his obsession with baseball cards and that weird hobby of collecting garden gnomes. Otherwise, I have to admit, he's a really good dad. And a generally all-around nice guy.

The Rodent (Matt McGuire)

My little brother is a 24/7 dweeb. He likes to entertain himself by switching my shampoo with hand lotion, stealing all of my shoes, and putting the dirty clothes in my hamper back on my hangers.

The best thing to do if you've got a spiky-haired pest of a brother bugging you: ignore him. But if you can't, here are my top tips for what to do with a little brother like mine:

Top Tips for Pest Control

- **Book the boy on that all-expenses-paid trip to Siberia he's always wanted.**
- **Tell your Gammy to come over with all of her photo albums, 'cause her adorable grandson wants to know all about his family history.**
- **Digitally doctor his photo, replacing the football in his arms with a "Sassy Sally" baby doll. Make a very large poster. Threaten to hang fifty copies all over his school if he messes with you. This will keep him in line for three to five days.**

People at School

Kate

She's pretty, she's popular, and she's just about the witchiest girl I've ever met (even though we actually used to be best friends—back before she grew five inches in one summer and started hanging with "the cool kids").

Tudgeman

He likes going on field trips, being in the Mathlete Club, and doing assignments for extra credit. There's something not quite right about Larry. . . .

Ethan

What's that? Do I hear a heavenly chorus? Beautiful harp music? Oh no, it's just Ethan passing by. Ethan is my crush-boy. All you need to remember about him is . . . sigh.

Mr. Pettus

A nice guy, even if he's got no eyebrows (one too many science class explosions). He also smells like cafeteria cheese, and is way too fond of field trips (blech)!

Mr. Dig

Our substitute teacher. He's kinda odd but definitely cool, too. He always tells you stuff that's true—and actually useful—even when it's so not in the lesson plan. How cool is that for a teacher?

Coach Kelly

Empress of the gym-nauseum, with all the sensitivity of an army drill sergeant. If she's not making you do deep knee bends till it hurts, she's teaching you how to square dance. 'Nuf said.

Monday

Dear Journal,

Finally! I'm finally popular! I've been invited to the social event of the season—Danny Kessler's pool party! Look, here's proof I'm not hallucinating—the invitation. Check it out.

Dear Lizy McGwire
You are invited to a...

POOL PARTY

this Saturday, 11 A.M. onwards
Snacks will be served

DRESS CODE = Bathing Suits

3242 Hillridge Lane

No Mathletes!!

See—that's me! That's my name right there. Okay, so they've totally misspelled it, but they're popular people. Stuff like spelling is only meant for us mortals.

No Mathletes. Wow. Cool kids only, right? And I'm invited, which means—I'm cool! This is totally going to be the Defining Moment of My Adolescence (or D.M.O.M.A. for short).

Wednesday

Dear Journal,

How could everything go so wrong? Suddenly, I'm not going to the pool party, but Miranda is, and my mom is angry with me. When did I fall through the looking glass?

I can't believe Nana McGuire's birthday is on the same day as the pool party. She's got 364 other days to have a birthday, but oooh no.

This is it: I'm missing the Defining Moment of My Adolescence! Everything will be different from now on . . . I'm an outcast.

D.M.O.M.A. Diagram:

Going to the World's Most Popular Pool Party.

But I can't go to the pool party.

Well, I guess the D.M.O.M.A. is learning that no one always gets what they want.

Yeah, that sounds pretty grown-up—hey, waitie just a sec . . . Miranda gets to go!

No fair!

But on the other hand, Gordo says he'll hang out with me on Saturday, and we'll tie-dye clothes and all kinds of fun stuff.

Okay, so I guess the D.M.O.M.A. is realizing there is no single D.M.O.M.A.

Whatever . . . I gotta go buy some dye. I'm outie!

Wednesday

Dear Journal,

Today was picture day—the day when your face gets immortalized for the yearbook, and is seen by everyone . . . forever . . . until the end of time. Augh!

First, my mom tried to make me look like a Cookie Elf by putting me in Nana McGuire's unicorn sweater. Which is fine if:

a. You like unicorns.

b. Your fashion sense has been surgically removed.

My actual school photo. Beautiful, isn't it?

So I manage to eject from that scenario, right in time for Kate to cover me in green paint. Why? Take your pick:

a. Kate was aiming for Miranda, to ruin her clothes, 'cause they were wearing the same outfit.

b. Kate's a witch.

I really have to plan ahead for next year's picture day . . . but what look should I go for?

Rock Star

Well, a skintight leopard-print suit would certainly get me noticed . . . by the 'rents! I doubt I'd even make it out of the house!

This is harder than I thought! Well, at least I know not to go for . . .

Good thing there's no fashion catwalk on picture day. I don't think I'd get very far in these heels.

I'll also be avoiding . . .

My Grade School Thanksgiving Costume

Giant pumpkin pies rarely get a second date.

But most of all, I'm not going to wear . . .

Anything My Dad Suggests

I refuse to take fashion tips from a man who wears bright orange Speedos to the beach. (The horror! The horror!)

Friday

Dear Journal,

This week reeked! First, I made a seriously complete fool of myself trying out for the Hillridge cheerleading squad—which, of course, I totally didn't make.

Then, while I was instant-messaging with Miranda, I accidentally sent an e-mail to the whole school insulting Kate, who DID make the squad (which still freaks me out).

And as if that wasn't bad enough, when the Queen of Mean found out about that accidental e-mail, she totally confronted me and Miranda—and when I choked in stark fear, Miranda took the rap for me.

Then, Kate started a "dirty tricks" war with my best bud that lasted all week long. Oh, why did I ever send that e-mail? I mean, if they didn't want me spreading malicious gossip around the school, why did they invent the Internet?

It's not my fault!

Miranda was such a good friend, pretending that she sent the e-mail. And I'm not just saying that 'cause she might put green dye in my hair spray. (Wow, she sure fights nasty for such a nice girl!)

Anyway, dyeing Kate's hair green was a pretty harsh practical joke, but in the end it turned out okay. I stood up to Kate and told her it was me who sent the insulting e-mail. I got Miranda off the hook, and everything returned to normal . . . except for that "very special" cheer that Kate and her new buds on the cheerleading squad made up to chant in front of the whole school at a pep rally at the end of the week:

U.G.L.Y.
You ain't got no alibi.
You ugly.
Yeah, yeah, you ugly.
(Repeat 3x)
2,4,6,8,
who's the girl we
love to hate?
Lizzie...Lizzie...
Big Loser!

Thank you SO much, Gordo, for writing the lyrics down on this napkin after school today. Otherwise, I might have forgotten about the total humiliation of having the entire school laugh hysterically at me.

Thursday

Dear Journal,

I'm on an overnight science class field trip at the moment, which is why these pages are a mess! This isn't just any old field trip, of course—it's the worst field trip in the entire history of science class field trips. And it could have been so different. Like, maybe a little romance with Ethan Craft, toasting s'mores over the fire and gazing at the stars. But what do I get instead? Mr. Pettus goes all Survivor once we get into Blair Witch country, and makes us do some creepy science competition between the girls and the boys. We have to identify as much nature stuff as possible in one afternoon—and the losing group has to dig up earthworms for the class worm farm. . . .

Hey, Mr. Pettus! Maybe you should watch a little less reality television?

But the worst part of all is that my mom is the chaperone! Can life BE any more embarrassing? The woman's obsessed with toilet paper, for one thing. And she brought this giant bag of it. I swear, I'd rather have the earth swallow me up than be on this trip now.

My Science Field Trip "Nature Specimens"

Okay, this is what us botanists call "grass."

And here's another blade of grass . . . but it's obviously completely different from the first. Gosh.

Er, this is a leaf. That's natural, right? Hmm, did I just see Ethan go by with a water gun? I better go investigate.

Monday

Dear Journal,

Here's a typical day in my absolutely thrilling life.

Class Schedule

Student: Lizzie McGuire

PERIOD	CLASS	TIME
HR	Home Room	9:00–9:30 a.m.
1st	Math	9:35–10:25 a.m.
2nd	Chemistry	10:30–11:20 a.m.
3rd	Gym nauseum	11:25–12:15 p.m.
4th	Lunch	12:20–1:10 p.m.
5th	Study Hall	1:15–2:05 p.m.
6th	English	2:10–3:00 p.m.
End of School Day		3:00 p.m.

Homeroom – 9:00-9:30 a.m.

Remember that I haven't brought my math homework in because Matt got peanut butter all over it. Get paranoid about flunking math.

First Period – Math – 9:35-10:25 a.m.

Spend the first fifteen minutes of the lesson worrying about my homework. Then realize today is Monday and it doesn't have to be in until Thursday. Kate, Queen of Mean, totally wipes out trying to do a quadratic equation in front of the class. She sees me snickering. Like I care.

Second Period – Chemistry – 10:30-11:20 a.m.

Mr. Pettus sets his lab coat on fire—for the sixth time this semester. Create a graph of how long it takes for oil to heat up to 400°. Class dismissed early due to terrible smell of hot oil and singed science teacher in classroom.

Third Period – Gym (nauseum) – 11:25-12:15 p.m.

Sit-ups and deep knee bends (ow, ow, ow), followed by dodgeball (ow! ow! ow!). Gawk at Ethan, just before I'm hit in the face by two balls at once. Kate and Claire claim it was an accident. Yeah, right. In the locker room, Miranda "accidentally" spills glue into their hair spray.

Fourth Period – Lunch – 12:20-1:10 p.m.

Ah, the social minefield! What to eat, where to sit? Wow, I'm glad I'm not a new kid: sit in the wrong place and you could be an outcast forever. Fortunately, I sit with Gordo and Miranda, which takes a lot of trouble out of it. Kate and Claire come in late with their hair still wet—they had to shower twice after gym class. Wonder why?

Fifth Period – Study Hall – 1:15-2:05 p.m.

Pass a note to Miranda to say I overheard Ethan say he's going to see a movie on Friday. Suggest to her that maybe we should go, too, and grab a seat behind him and then tap him on the shoulder and say, like, "Omigosh! You're here, too?" Sneak a final look to see if Ethan's looking at me now.

Sixth Period – English – 2:10-3:00 p.m.

We're studying To Kill a Mockingbird. Ethan has some problems with it—he's confused because there aren't any mockingbirds in the book. Still, he looks sooo cute when he furrows his brow.

3:00 p.m. – End of School Day

I'm outie! Head on over to Miranda's to do homework and watch a DVD. Gordo's coming over later, and we'll get some pizza. Hey, with best buds like the ones I've got, my life's not bad at all!

Tuesday

Dear Journal,

All right! Finally, a little responsibility around here! Mom and Dad are going out to dinner on Friday, and I'm going to look after Matt while they're out. Mom said I have to be fully prepared for any emergency if I want to babysit Matt, but I think I've got everything covered:

Yeah, and I get to boss Matt around too—officially! Oops, did I just say that out loud?

My Babysitting Emergency List

- A big bowl of popcorn
- Miranda and Gordo to keep me company
- One-way ticket to Peru! Buh-bye, Toad Boy!

Friday night

Dear Journal,

Omigosh! This isn't happening! Someone is trying to break into the house RIGHT NOW! I'm writing this down in the event that Matt and I are killed by a rampaging ax murderer . . . sort of our last words. I'll have to keep it short—Matt shut off the power, but there's definitely someone trying to break into the house.

I have to keep it short—the prowler might break in any minute now. If my last journal entry reads "I think I can hear someone coming in through

AARRGGHH . . . !"

Like I'll have time to write "AARRGGHH" down.

then you'll know what happened.

Hey! What am I doing sitting here cowering like an overpaid starlet in a teen horror flick? I'm in charge here, and I'm not going down without a fight. Okay, Mr. Prowler . . . you asked for it!

Friday night, much later

Dear Journal,

Okay, so Mr. Prowler is better known as "my dad." Me? Overreacting? Never.

Monday

Dear Journal,

The elections for school president are coming up, and the candidates have announced themselves. I'm not sure why they bothered. I mean—a choice between the Claire Witch Project and Larry Tudgeman?

Wow, talk about being caught between a geek and a hard place.

You know, maybe I should listen to Gordo's advice and run for office. Hmm, I think I could really make a difference. They do say "power corrupts," but I'm sure that won't happen to me.

Wednesday

Dear Journal,

Gordo's my campaign manager. He's suggested I schmooze the dorkestra, Mathletes, foreign exchange kids—everyone Claire and her friends snub. He also thinks I could get votes from the "second-tier" popular kids like the Drama Groupies. He may have a point.

Friday

Dear Journal,

I'm busy, busy, busy! Giving speeches, shaking hands. The geeky kids love me. And, I can't believe it, but the Drama Groupies actually invited me to hang with them. They're soooo cool. Was supposed to go over to Miranda's tonight, but the drama kids are hanging out at the mall.

Monday

Dear Journal,

Next Monday is election day—and my campaign rocks! I just may win this thing! But don't worry, I won't forget the little people like Gordo and . . . er . . . what's-her-name. No time to talk—I'm on a roll!

Thursday

Dear Journal,

Gordo forgot to pick up my dry cleaning—do I have to do everything around here? Where is Miranda with my double-tall skinny decaf cappuccino? Why am I surrounded by incompetents? The election is on Monday—I'm sooo gonna win! I could never lose in a million years! Who wouldn't vote for me?

Monday (Election Day)

Dear Journal,

Arrrrrrrgggggh! I can't believe I lost to Larry Tudgeman! How on earth did he get elected, with that bizarre election manifesto?

Welcome to my personal nightmare.

Larry Tudgeman's Manifesto

- i promise to eat a worm for every vote i get.
- in the event that i run out of worms, acorns may be permitted as a suitable alternative.
- Everyone in school will be assigned a Star Wars nickname (FYi—Han Solo is already taken).
- Gym will be replaced with Dwarflord class.
- The school cafeteria will start selling toothpaste sandwiches.

Monday

Dear Journal,

Hey—it's our big social studies experiment tomorrow. We all get "married off" and get jobs assigned to us. It could be pretty cool! I'd like to know what the future holds for me, and what kind of career I'll have. Hmm, I wonder who'll get paired with me?

Tuesday

Dear Journal,

I'm a lawyer! And I'm married to Gordo, which seems weird, but I should at least get a good grade out of it. His job is garbage collector. (Don't even go there.) But you should have seen Kate when it turned out she was "marrying" Tudgeman. That wiped the smug "I'm a TV anchorwoman" smirk off her face!

Guess who Miranda got paired up with? I'll give you a clue—his name is Ethan Craft! And Ethan's job is—get this—surgeon. Hmm.

Oh, well. Guess I better get started on my "law career."

I, Lizzie McGuire, district attorney of Hillridge, do solemnly swear to pass the following legislation:

By order of the District Attorney's office:

* All little brothers are to be fitted with a mute button.
* Accessorizing is to be put on the National Curriculum.
* Mothers are to be limited to three embarrassing comments per day.
* Catty remarks are to be punishable by eight years imprisonment (that's right, Kate).
* The following colors for fathers' "holiday pants" are now banned: lemon yellow, bright red, turquoise, or anything that could be described as "groovy."

Friday

Dear Journal,

Uh-oh, I can't believe Kate and Ethan are plotting together! They're married to other people, but Kate's asking Ethan to leave Miranda! Think of the children! And after Miranda worked nights at the diner to put Ethan through medical school! I've got to tell her as soon as possible. And poor Larry—all that overtime he put in to get Kate that desperately needed plastic surgery and psychotherapy. Kate and Ethan: you're heartless!

Tuesday

Dear Journal,

Well, I guess not every relationship lasts. In fact, according to our experiment, none of them did. But I do kind of wonder what happened to our future selves after we all got divorced . . . .

- **Kate: Lost her job as a TV anchorwoman when her stress rash returned. Now works as a bouncer on Jerry Springer.**
- **Gordo: Transferred to Sewage, and eventually found the lost city of Atlantis underneath Milwaukee. Who knew?**
- **Miranda: Went on to make the World's Largest Flan for 50,000 people in NYC's Central Park. Unfortunately, they'd all filled up on bread beforehand.**
- **And Lizzie McGuire: Hey, who knows? Stick around, why don't you?**

Thursday

Dear Journal,

I'm in English class pretending to read some dorky play, but I've just got to tell you about the terrible dream I had last night. I dreamed that Matt took the wrong bus to school, and ended up at Hillridge Junior High. And the funny thing was, Ethan thought he was really cool, and Matt kept making up these outrageous stories and everyone just ate it up!

ARRRRRGH! I can't believe Matt is such a big hit at school! How can anyone believe all the stupid stories he makes up?

Lies Matt Has Told

- **Having the Death Star explode at the end of Star Wars was his idea.**
- **He'll be sharing more recipes on his talk show next week.**
- **He invented the question mark.**
- **He's illustrated over 200 issues of Superman.**
- **He has two hearts, allowing him to hold his breath for up to fifteen minutes.**
- **He was brought up by wolves. (Actually, i'd believe that one if i didn't know better. . . .)**

I was sooo busy watching out for Claire and Kate, it never occurred to me that Matt might become the most popular person at school—who could have seen that one coming? I mean, what's he got that Kate doesn't?

Apart from an allergy to soap and water?

	Kate	Matt
Special Abilities	**Accessorizes her accessories**	**irritates even more than poison ivy**
Background	**Daughter of a cheerleader, granddaughter of a cheerleader**	**Heir to the Lost Throne of Moldova (apparently)**
Appeal	**Popular, blond, tall cheerleader. Need i say more?**	**Why are people drawn to car crashes?**
Style	**Middle-of-the-road, play-it-safe, just-the-same-as-everyone-else clothes**	**Style? His specialty is belching the alphabet up to Q. You must be kidding.**

Well, there are two ways to solve this little problem:

- **The first way is to sit down with Matt, have a good heart-to-heart, and try and understand him better, so we both get along in this school.**
- **The second way is to call the cops, and have him taken off to his own school. Hmm, which to go for? Thinking, thinking. . . . (What was that number again? 9-1-something?)**

Tuesday

Dear Journal,

It's 2:30 in the morning, but I just can't sleep—there's too much to think about. Since Miranda and I helped out with that volunteer recycling project at school, I've been totally freaking about recycling and food banks and saving the Earth. So, I've made a big decision—I'm going to recycle more, learn more about the planet . . . and stop eating meat. Gordo and Miranda don't seem to understand, and Miranda says I'm getting obsessive. Obsessive! I <u>cannot</u> believe her! So I can't sleep. So I think and worry about this stuff 24/7, so what! It's important! What does Miranda know?

- A piece of the rain forest the size of Washington, D.C., is chopped down every day.
- Over 30,000 gallons of water are wasted by Americans every single day!
- In the U.S.A., each man, woman, and child uses 440 lbs of packaging per year—which is just thrown away.
- 99 percent of all paper products are recyclable—but only 15 percent of people recycle!

I mean, check this out. (Don't worry about my wasting paper, I recycled a piece of a brown grocery bag.)

Now if that doesn't make us think, then what will? But what can the average person do? Just look! I have another list. (This one I wrote on a Burger Buddy bag I snatched from my father before he tossed it. Note to self: talk to Dad about giving up burgers, like me.)

- **Start a recycling program at your school—paper is easiest to start with. Most recycling companies will come in to talk to your class!**
- **Don't pester your folks to give you a lift to the mall—try walking or taking the bus. Car exhaust fumes count for 75 percent of all air pollution today!**
- **Bring a reusable tote bag to the supermarket, and try to reuse stuff wherever you can.**
- **Get a group of friends together to pick up litter in a nearby park.**

Hey . . . (yawn) . . . that's a pretty good start! (yawn) . . . if only I weren't so tired . . . I could come up with the perfect recycling solution . . . (yawn) . . . wow, that Burger Buddy bag still smells like the burger that was in it . . . oh, man, I forgot how good burgers smell (yawwwn). . . maybe I'll give up meat next week . . .

zzzzzzzzzzzzzzzzzzzzzzzzz.

Monday

Dear Journal,

I can hardly believe it, but Gordo went out on a date last night . . . with Brooke Baker, no less! I've gotta admit, I can't believe Brooke likes Gordo. Sure, he's a nice guy, but that doesn't mean he's boyfriend material!

Look, it's not the fact that he's going out with a beautiful, popular girl that's bothering me . . . it's that he lied to Miranda and me.

Yep, that's it. That's the reason all right. Sure it is.

Okay, okay, so maybe I'm just missing something about Gordo. Maybe he's more attractive than I think. Like, maybe he's Spider-Man, and I just can't see beyond Peter Parker.

McGuire, you're getting weird.

Head: So what's in here that Brooke might find so attractive? Okay, he's kind and considerate—and always thinking of his friends. Though actually, a lot of the time he's thinking of weird things like haikus, or Hungarian house music . . . so that might count against him. Overall though, he's pretty cool, and really smart. Not bad, I guess. . . .

Mouth: Well, he generally has interesting things to say . . . but again, he does come out with some weird stuff occasionally, like:

- **Man is born free, but everywhere he lives in chains. Or duplexes.**
- **What is the sound of one hand clapping? Can you dance to it?**
- **If a tree falls on a car in the forest and no one hears it, does my father's insurance still go up?**

Hands: Not much going on here, except they're good for making models with. And tie-dyeing sheets. Oh, and making papier-mâché stuff—he's really good at that, too. And making mix tapes—and generally helping out. But apart from that, not much.

Feet: Well, these are good for playing Hacky Sack with, but not much else. They take him to the library a lot, which is why he's so well-read; and they take him to museums, which is why he's so smart; and concerts, too. Of course, they also take him to supersecret romantic rendezvous with Brooke Baker. . . .

So, to sum up: Gordo's kind and considerate, he's a good conversationalist, he's good at making stuff and helping people out, he's well-read, knows about lots of cool stuff, and isn't bad looking . . . so a girl wouldn't be interested in that, right? Right? Well, whatever. I'm sure Miranda can find a way to convince Gordo we're just not ready for him to have a girlfriend. No way.

Tuesday

Dear Journal,

Check it out! I've got one of Ethan's test papers! That's right, I've got something that Ethan has touched! Admittedly, he did throw it away, but it's still his. Mind you, if I only got a 10 out of 100 on my math quiz, I'd bury it in the backyard!

Math Quiz
20 Questions, 5 Points Each

F!
10/100

Name: Ethan Craft

Period: 1st.

I am so totally hot. Does it really matter that fractions aren't my forte?

1. Q: What is one half of one quarter?

   Is it 26?

2. Q: What do you get when you divide two thirds by one sixth?

   A headache?

3. Q: What is the common denominator of 6 and 9?

   Why is this on a math test? Isn't this a social studies question?

4. Q: Multiply two sevenths by one half.

Is that a cow? Clearly, Ethan needs help. <u>My</u> help!

5. Q: Which is greater: a half of five sevenths, or a quarter of an eighth?

   The last one?

Friday

Dear Journal,

Yes! The best thing that could have happened has happened! That's right, Ethan wants me to tutor him in math! Can you believe it? It's a dream come true! Ethan and I are going to be cozying up over equations, and giggling over geometry. I can see it now!

But how am I going to make fractions easy for Ethan? He won't be interested . . . he's only interested in brainless cheerleaders like Kate. . . . Hey, hold the phone! Maybe I've been going at this the wrong way. Maybe he has got some smarts, but I just need to get him interested first.

Okay, say we want to divide 2/3 by 3/4—all you have to do is take the 3/4, flip it over, then multiply the two figures together! Sounds hard? Not when you add . . . cheerleading power!

So now you've got eight out of nine cheerleaders, or eight ninths of a squad! I'm a genius! He's gonna love this!

I can't wait to try this out!

Tuesday

Dear Journal,

Hey, hey, hey! Things are looking up for once! Ethan thinks I'm cool because I found a way to teach him about fractions!

So now he's invited me to go bowling this Friday! Well, not just me, unfortunately, some of his friends will be there—and Miranda and Gordo have been invited, too. But he's still sort of asked me out. I kind of look at it as a date, just with lots of other people around! I just hope I don't embarrass myself.

Actually, one person who might embarrass me is Gordo. He's not exactly the world's best bowler. In fact, he's pretty much the world's worst bowler. I mean, there are people who get low scores, there are people who only ever bowl gutterballs . . . and then there are people whose fingers swell up so much that they have to have the ball cut off their hand. Can anyone guess what type Gordo is?

Attack of the Killer Bowling Ball

(Hmm—I better ask Miranda to give him some help.) But really, everything is way cool. What could possibly go wrong now? Uh-oh—better go. I can hear my dad coming up the stairs. . . .

Wednesday

Dear Journal,

I can't believe it! Dad came up to my room, and he was all "Let's spend some time together, Lizzie." And he told me he arranged our "father-daughter" night for Friday! But then Miranda reminded me that Friday is my sort-of-date bowling-with-Ethan night! So I canceled on my dad, but now I feel awful!

Oh, why is my dad doing this to me?! He's gotten all needy, on top of already being a world-class champion at Lizzie embarrassing. I mean, what was it I overheard him saying to Mom? "I am right on with the kids—I am the real Sam Shady."

Hmm—so he's embarrassing and lame . . . but (sigh) I guess I wouldn't exchange him for the world. In fact, perhaps there's a solution in there somewhere. We could do our father-daughter night out . . . at Ethan's bowling alley.

Monday

Dear Journal,

There's Kate Moss, Tyra Banks, Giselle—and now me! That's right, dear Journal, last week I entered Teen Attitude magazine's model search at the mall, and they signed me up! So now I'm striking poses, looking into the distance, and getting ready for my photo shoot!

No kidding. After my fashion show at the mall, the Teen Attitude magazine person called me a natural and gave me a modeling contract. There'll be more fashion shows in my future—and maybe even a cover shoot! I can see me now.

Another cool thing that happened: right after last week's fashion show, this ultrapopular girl named Jessica invited me to her dad's country club over the weekend! Whoo-hoo! Can you say "social promotion"? I was totally in the zone—and so were my buds, 'cause I made sure Miranda and Gordo got an invite, too.

A few weird things did happen to me today at school, though: Kate started talking to me again, and then she said, "Well, whatever you wear, Lizzie, everyone will be wearing tomorrow." How odd is that? Me—a fashion icon? I don't think so! And I noticed a lot of people in the hall staring at me. Like STARING. It was creepy. And then, when I said hi to Ethan, he got all weird and tongue-tied and ran away from me. . . .

Could it be my deodorant?

Wednesday

Dear Journal,

Okay—this is getting scary. Now Gordo and Miranda are acting all weird, too. Hanging on my every word, asking what they can do for me, arranging my "appearances" at popular people's parties. They're not my friends anymore . . . they're my "people." Yuck!

I spoke to Mr. Dig about it, and he recommends that I start acting like a real prima donna—then maybe my friends will realize how bad things have gotten.

MMM&M McGUIRE, McGUIRE, McGUIRE, AND McGUIRE
ENTERTAINMENT ATTORNEYS-AT-LAW

Contract of Employment

This contract is hereby drawn up between Ms. Lizzie McGuire (hereafter known as the Glamorous Celebrity) and Ms. Miranda Sanchez and Mr. David Gordon (hereafter known as the Lackeys).

Section 3, subsection 2

The Lackeys will be at the beck and call of the Glamorous Celebrity and will ensure:

* All social and business meetings are noted in a diary and attended on time.
* The Glamorous Celebrity will be protected from the "less popular" crowds.
* The Glamorous Celebrity dislikes green M&Ms, so they will be removed from the candy dish by hand.
* The Glamorous Celebrity will never have to do her own homework again.
* Matt will be placed inside an airtight container and floated out to sea.
* The Lackeys will sing and dance and bark like dogs on demand for the Glamorous Celebrity's amusement.
* The Lackeys will not speak until spoken to. Spontaneous gasps of admiration will, however, be permitted between the hours of 2 and 3 p.m. daily.
* On the first Wednesday of each month, the Lackeys will wash the car of the Glamorous Celebrity. (Until the Glamorous Celebrity actually owns a car, the Lackeys will come by and wash the driveway.)
* Upon arriving in any room, the Lackeys will throw rose petals before the Glamorous Celebrity, while singing, "You're Simply the Best."

Right. So if Miranda and Gordo want to act like my agents, they're gonna have to sign a contract. A nightmare contract! (Moo-ha-ha-ha!)

Tuesday

Dear Journal,

No time to talk—I'm in training! Yep, that's right, gotta exercise that old gray matter, because Gordo, Miranda, and I are entering the school's Fact-A-thlon . . . and we're gonna win that trip to Miami.

Fact-A-thlon? Did I overdose on geek pills during the night?

We're training with Mr. Dig, who's got this really weird way of teaching stuff. He's almost making learning fun! But Gordo is worried that we're not learning enough facts and figures and stuff (because that's the kind of guy he is), so I've decided to give my brain a pop quiz. Let's see if I can remember the most trivial pieces of information about everyone I know. That way I'll have both bases covered!

Miranda:

- Her favorite dessert is flan.
- Her worst fear is being locked in a closet full of Chihuahuas.
- She has a great singing voice.
- She uses Arm & Hammer toothpaste.
- Her middle name is isabelle.

Gordo:

- He weighs 116 pounds soaking wet.
- Both his parents are psychiatrists . . . and they never agree on anything.
- He used to be scared of falling down the bath drain when he was little.
- He knows all the atomic elements . . . and will sing them in a song if you give him any encouragement.
- His middle name is Zephyr.

Ethan:

- He is five hunky feet and ten gorgeous inches tall.
- He always wears white sports socks with two blue bands at the ankle.
- You cannot see into his room from the street using binoculars (because tree branches get in the way).
- He can throw a football over a hundred feet.
- He is really, really, really, really cute.

Hey—I rock at this! This quiz should be a breeze! Miami, here I come!

Wednesday

Dear Journal,

Shhh! Don't make a sound! I'm hiding out at Miranda's. Why am I being so quiet? Because I'm on the run!

In the last 24 hours my life has turned completely upside down. First, I found out someone had a crush on me, then I found out that it was Larry Tudgeman! Then we went on a date together. This all happened so quickly, I just found time to write about it now.

Hey–somewhere out there, in a parallel dimension, there's a Lizzie who is the most popular girl in school, who is going out with Ethan, has non-embarrassing parents and has a little brother who adores her. Arrrrrgh! I hate her already!

Top 3 Things i never expected to hear:

3. Matt: **"i'm sorry, Lizzie, i'll never bother you again."**

2. Mom: **"Let's not have a b-i-i-i-g talk about this, Lizzie, i'm sure you can handle it."**

1. Anyone: **"Hey, Lizzie, the Tudge has a colossal crush on you."**

So, pretty weird, huh? Obviously, once again we have entered the Bizarre Reverso World of Lizzie McGuire, where everything is the opposite of what you think.

Okay—so here's what happened. Not only did Larry have a crush on me, he then went and asked me out on a date. (I should've known something was up—he wasn't wearing his putty-colored shirt with the lime-green collar like he usually does.)

So, he asked me out on a date, and before I'd had a chance to stuff my brain back into my head, I heard myself saying "yes"! What's going on here?

And here we get to the very heart of weirdness: I actually had a pretty good time! Larry turned out to be an okay guy, and a lot cooler than I thought. He does what he wants, when he wants, and he doesn't worry about what anyone thinks. It just goes to show, you really shouldn't jump to conclusions about people!

The only thing is, I think Larry wants to be my boyfriend, and although I like him, I don't want that. So I was thinking of breaking it to him gently . . . but I haven't decided how yet. Here are some possibilites:

- **Missing school for the next week (attending via walkie-talkie held by Miranda)**
- **Pretending i've transferred to the National Sled Dog Mushing Academy in Alaska**
- **Pretending i've got amnesia ("You want to go out with who, Larry?")**

Or I guess I could just be straight, and break it to him gently. Could I? Hmm—we'll have to see what tomorrow brings. . . .

Thursday

Dear Journal,

Whew! Things are back on track again! I managed to break the news to Larry gently. In fact, he took it really well . . . I mean really well. He even started asking about Miranda! In fact, I actually started thinking, "What's wrong with me, Larry?"

I spoke to Ethan again today, and you'll be pleased to hear that he's still really cute! And, better than that, he still thinks I'm really cool. All that help that I gave him with math really paid off—he told me he's still "acing" his math tests.

The great thing about Ethan is that he's not judgmental—he's pretty much okay with everybody. Actually, this can be a bad thing, as well as good, because it means he doesn't notice what a witch Kate is most of the time. I can't understand why he can't see Kate is the original Queen of Mean—it's common knowledge, like the fact that cafeteria food sucks, Larry will eat paste if it's left out, and Gordo will always have something to say that's really difficult to understand.

? → ~~Mrs. Ethan Craft~~

Lizzie McGuire-Craft

~~Lizzie Craft~~

Ethan McGuire ← YES!

Hey—when Ethan and I get married, I wonder if I'm going to take his name. I better get that figured out before we send out the invites.

saturday

Dear Journal,

something's up—I actually found Toad Boy in my room yesterday, and when I asked him what he was doing, he said he just came up to borrow a "hair scrunchie"! Now come on!

The best thing to do with a little brother like Matt is just ignore him, I think . . . but it's very difficult to ignore someone who might possibly put a hornet's nest in your underwear drawer . . . I just don't trust that little rodent-faced pest . . .

Ooooh—hello there I'm Lizzie and this is my secret diary—I'm going to put all my secret thoughts into it, which are completely lame and boring.

wow—how can a secret diary be so geeky? where are all the secret codes, writing in invisible ink, and hidden compartments?

why does she keep going on about Ethan? She's such a dork. I was hoping for some really cool stuff or at least something I could blackmail Lizzie with . . .

but she really does have the most boring life in the world. Not like me! My life is great!

Now what else should a really cool diary have in it? Oh yeah! Since I'm a master of the unarmed arts, I should really give you some top Ninja tips on how to annoy your sister. So here they are:

- The Sneaking Snake: Creep into your sister's room when she's out with her dorky friends and write lots of stuff in her diary.
- The Alaska Shower: Wait until your sister is in the shower, then sneak down to the basement and turn off all the hot water. Don't forget to listen to her scream.
- The Invisible Pack Rat: Hide your sister's favorite pair of shoes. Never tell her where they are. Bury them in the garden if necessary.
- The Forgetful Parrot: Answer the telephone for your sister. Act like you are taking detailed messages but actually do not write down a thing.

Wow—I could write a lot more, but I am running out of room . . .

What the?! . . . That's it! That's the last straw! I'm gonna annihilate the little freak! I thought he'd been acting really suspicious recently, and now I know why!

Well, I was almost done with this journal anyway, and my second journal can begin with a very happy story . . . the story of how I got my revenge on Toad Boy! Stay tuned!

—Love, Lizzie